EV ES
HORRID HENRY!

Libraries, books and more...........

e
s
t
)-

ch
s

Please return/renew this item by the last date due.
Library items may also be renewed by phone on
030 33 33 1234 (24hours) or via our website

www.cumberland.gov.uk/libraries-and-archives

HORRID HENRY

ROCK STAR

FRANCESCA SIMON

ILLUSTRATED BY TONY ROSS

Orion

For Jesse Nunn, a major league Horrid Henry fan, and for Imogen Stubbs

ORION CHILDREN'S BOOKS

First published in Great Britain in 2010 as
"Horrid Henry Rocks" by Orion Children's Books
This edition published in 2019 by Hodder and Stoughton

7 9 10 8

Text © Francesca Simon 2010
Illustrations © Tony Ross 2010
Additional images © Shutterstock

The rights of Francesca Simon and Tony Ross to be identified as author and
illustrator of this work have been asserted.

A CIP catalogue record for this book is available from the British Library.

ISBN 978 1 84255 134 9

Printed and bound in Great Britain by Clays Ltd, Elcograf S.P.A.

The paper and board used in this book are from well-managed forests and other
responsible sources.

MIX
Paper from
responsible sources
FSC® C104740

Orion Children's Books
An imprint of
Hachette Children's Group
Part of Hodder and Stoughton
Carmelite House
50 Victoria Embankment
London EC4Y 0DZ

An Hachette UK Company
www.hachette.co.uk

www.hachettechildrens.co.uk
www.horridhenry.co.uk

CONTENTS

HORRID HENRY'S

INVASION

"BAA! BAA! BAA!"

Perfect Peter baaed happily at his sheep collection. There they were, his ten lovely little *sheepies*, all beautifully lined up from **biggest** to SMALLEST, heads facing forward, fluffy tails against the wall, all five centimetres apart from one another, all—

Perfect Peter gasped. Something was wrong. Something was TERRIBLY wrong. But what? What? Peter scanned the mantelpiece. Then he saw . . .

NOoOOo!

FLUFF PUFF, his favourite sheep,
the one with the pink and yellow
nose, was facing the wrong way
round. His nose was **shoved** against
the wall. His tail was facing forward.
And he was . . . he was . . . crooked!

This could only mean . . . this could
only mean . . .

"Mum!" screamed Peter. "Mum!
Henry's been in my room again!"

"HENRY!" shouted Mum. "Keep out of
Peter's room."

"I'm not in Peter's room," yelled
Horrid Henry. "I'm in mine."

"But he was," wailed Peter.

"Wasn't!" bellowed Horrid Henry.

Tee hee.

Horrid Henry was strictly forbidden to go into Peter's bedroom without **Peter's** permission. But sometimes, thought Horrid Henry, when Peter was being even more of a *toady toad* than usual, he had no choice but to invade.

Peter had run blabbing to Mum that Henry had watched **Mutant Max** and **Knight Fight** when Mum had said he could only watch one or the other. Henry had been banned from watching TV all day. Peter was such a *telltale* **frogface** ninnyhammer **toady** POO BAG, thought Horrid Henry grimly. Well, just wait till Peter tried to colour in his new picture, he'd—

"MUM!" screamed Peter. "Henry switched the caps on my coloured pens. I just put pink in the sky."

"DIDN'T!" yelled Henry.

"Did!" wailed Peter.

"Prove it," said Horrid Henry, smirking.

Mum came upstairs. Quickly Henry

leapt over the mess covering the floor of his room, **flopped** on his bed and grabbed a **Screamin' Demon** comic. Peter came and stood in the doorway.

"Henry's being **HORRID**," snivelled Peter.

"Henry, have you been in Peter's room?" said Mum.

Henry sighed loudly. "Of course I've been in his **smelly** room. I live here, don't I?"

"I mean when he wasn't there," said Mum.

"No," said Horrid Henry. This wasn't a lie, because even if Peter wasn't there his **HORRIBLE** *stinky* smell was.

"He has too," said Peter. "**FLUFF PUFF** was turned the wrong way round."

"Maybe he was just trying to escape from your **pongy pants**," said Henry. "I would."

"Mum!" said Peter.

"Henry! Don't be **HORRID**. Leave your brother alone."

"I am leaving him alone," said Horrid Henry. "Why can't he leave me alone? And get out of my room, Peter!" he shrieked, as Peter put his foot just inside Henry's door.

Peter quickly withdrew his foot.

Henry *glared* at Peter.

Peter *glared* at Henry.

Mum sighed. "The next one who goes into the other's room without permission will be banned from the

COMPUTER for a week. And no
pocket money either."

She turned to go.

Henry stuck out his tongue at Peter.

"Telltale," he mouthed.

"Mum!" screamed Peter.

Perfect Peter stalked back to his
bedroom. How dare Henry sneak
in and mess up his sheep? What a
MEAN, HORRIBLE brother. Perhaps
he needed to calm down and listen
to a little music. The Daffy and her

Dancing Daisies Greatest Hits CD
always cheered him up.

"Dance and prance.
Prance and dance.
You say moo moo. We say baa.
Everybody says moo moo baa baa,"
piped Perfect Peter as he put on the
Daffy CD.

"BOILS ON YOUR FAT FACE
BOILS MAKE YOU DUMB.
CHOP CHOP CHOP 'EM OFF
STICK 'EM ON YOUR BUM!"

blared the CD player.

Huh? What was that **HORRIBLE** song? Peter yanked out the CD. It was the **Skullbangers** singing the horrible "**BONY BOIL**" song. Henry must have sneaked a **Skullbanger** CD inside the Daffy case. How dare he? How dare he? Peter would storm straight downstairs and tell Mum. Henry would get into big trouble. **BIG BIG TROUBLE**.

Then Peter paused. There was the TEENY-TINY possibility that Peter had mixed them up by mistake . . . No. He needed absolute proof of

Henry's **HORRIDNESS**. He'd do his homework, then have a good look around Henry's room to see if his Daffy CD was hidden there.

Peter glanced at his "To Do" list, pinned on his noticeboard. When he'd written it that morning it read:

Peter's To Do List
Practise cello
Fold clothes and put away
Do homework
Brush my teeth
Read Bunny's Big Boo Boo

The list now read:

Peter's To Do List
Practise ~~cello~~ belly dancing
unFold clothes and ~~put~~ away
throw
Don't ~~Do~~ homework
~~Flush~~ my teeth ~~down the toilet~~
Read Bunny's Big ~~Poo~~ Poo

At the bottom someone had added:

Pick my nose
Pinch mum
Give Henry all my money

Well, here was proof! He was going to go straight down and tell on Henry.

"Mum! Henry's been in my room again. He scribbled all over my To Do list."

"**HENRY!**" screamed Mum. "I am sick and tired of this! Keep out of your brother's bedroom! This is your last warning! No playing on the computer for a week!"

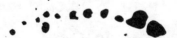

SNEAK. SNEAK. SNEAK.

Horrid Henry slipped inside

the enemy's bedroom. He'd pay Peter
back for getting him banned from the
computer.

There was Peter's cello. **HA!** It was
the work of a moment to unwind all
the strings. Now, what else, what else?
He could *switch* around Peter's pants
and sock drawers.

NO! Even better. Quickly Henry
undid all of Peter's socks, and
mismatched them. Who said socks
should match?

TEE HEE. Peter would go **MAD** when
he found out he was wearing one

Sammy the Snail sock with one **Daffy** sock. Then Henry snatched **BUNNYKINS** off Peter's bed and crept out.

SNEAK. SNEAK. SNEAK.

Perfect Peter crept down the hall and stood outside Henry's bedroom, holding a **MUDDY TWIG**. His heart was **POUNDING**. Peter knew he was strictly forbidden to go into Henry's room without permission. But Henry kept breaking that rule. So why shouldn't he?

Squaring his shoulders, Peter tiptoed in.

Crunch.
Crunch.
Crunch.

Henry's room was a pigsty, thought Perfect Peter, wading through broken knights, crumpled sweet wrappers, dirty clothes, ripped comics and muddy shoes.

Mr Kill. He'd steal Mr Kill. HA!

Serve Henry right. And he'd put the
MUDDY TWIG in Henry's bed. Serve him
double right. Perfect Peter **grabbed**
Mr Kill, shoved the twig in Henry's
bed and nipped back to his room.
And **SCREAMED**.

FLUFF PUFF wasn't just turned
the wrong way, he was – **GONE!**

Henry must have stolen him. And Lambykins was gone too. And Squish. Peter only had seven sheep left.

And where was his **BUNNYKINS?** He wasn't on the bed where he belonged. No!!!!!! This was the last straw. This was **war**.

The coast was clear. Peter always took ages having his bath. **Horrid Henry** slipped into the **worm's** room.

He'd pay Peter back for stealing **Mr Kill**. There he was, **shoved** at the top of Peter's wardrobe, where Peter always hid things he didn't want Henry to find. Well, **HA HA HA**, thought Horrid Henry, rescuing Mr Kill.

Now what to do, what to do? Horrid Henry *scooped* up all of Peter's remaining sheep and **shoved** them inside Peter's pillowcase.

What else? Henry glanced round Peter's immaculate room. He could mess it up. Nah, thought Henry. Peter loved tidying. He could — aha.

Peter had pinned drawings all over the wall above his bed. Henry surveyed them. Shame, thought Henry, that Peter's pictures were all so dull. I mean, really, "My Family", and "MY BUNNYKINS". **Horrid Henry** climbed on Peter's bed to reach the drawings.

Poor Peter, thought Horrid Henry. What a TERRIBLE artist he was. No wonder he was such a **smelly toad** if he had to look at such **AWFUL** pictures all the time. Perhaps Henry could improve them . . .

Now, let's see, thought **Horrid Henry**, getting out some crayons. Drawing a crown on my head would be a big improvement. There! That livens things up. And a **BIG RED NOSE** on Peter would help, too, thought Henry, drawing away. So would a **droopy** moustache on Mum. And as for that stupid picture of **BUNNYKINS**, well, why not draw

a lovely toilet for him to—

"What are you doing in here?" came a little voice.

Horrid Henry turned.

There was Peter, in his bunny pyjamas, glaring at him.

Uh oh. If Peter told on him again, Henry would be in **BIG, BIG, MEGA-BIG TROUBLE**. Mum would probably ban him from the **COMPUTER** for ever.

"You're in my room. I'm telling on you," shrieked Peter.

"Shhh!" hissed Horrid Henry.

"What do you mean, shhh?" said

Peter. "I'm going straight down to tell Mum."

"One word and you're **DEAD**, worm," said Horrid Henry. "Quick! Close the door."

Perfect Peter looked behind him. "Why?"

"Just do it, **worm**," hissed Henry.

Perfect Peter shut the door.

"What are you doing?" he demanded.

"Dusting for fingerprints," said Horrid Henry *smoothly*.

Fingerprints?

"What?" said Peter.

"I thought I heard someone in your room, and ran in to check you were okay. Just look what I found," said Horrid Henry dramatically, pointing to Peter's now empty mantelpiece.

Peter let out a squeal.

"My sheepies!" wailed Peter.

"I think there's a burglar in the house," whispered Horrid Henry urgently. "And I think he's hiding . . .

in your room."

Peter gulped. A burglar? In his room?

"A burglar?"

"Too right," said Henry. "Who do you think stole BUNNYKINS? And all your sheep?"

"You," said Peter.

Horrid Henry snorted. "No! What would I want with your STUPID sheep? But a sheep rustler would love them."

Perfect Peter hesitated. Could Henry be telling the truth? Could a burglar really have stolen his sheep?

"I think he's hiding under the bed," hissed Horrid Henry. "Why don't you check?"

Peter stepped back.

"No," said Peter. "I'm scared."

"Then get out of here as quick as you can," whispered Henry. "I'll check."

"Thank you, Henry," said Peter.

Perfect Peter crept into the hallway. Then he stopped. Something wasn't right . . . something was a little bit wrong.

Perfect Peter **MARCHED** back into his bedroom. Henry was by the door.

"I think the burglar is hiding in your wardrobe, I'll get—"

"You said you were fingerprinting," said Peter suspiciously. "With what?"

"My fingers," said Horrid Henry. "Why do you think it's called fingerprinting?"

Then Peter caught sight of his drawings.

"You've **RUINED** my pictures!"

shrieked Peter.

"It wasn't me, it must have been the burglar," said Horrid Henry.

"You're trying to **trick** me," said Peter. "I'm telling!"

Time for Plan B.

"I'm only in here 'cause you were in my room," said Henry.

"Wasn't!"

"Were!"

"Liar!"

"Liar!"

"You stole BUNNYKINS!"

"You stole Mr Kill!"

"Thief!"

"Thief!"

"I'm telling on you."

"I'm telling on you!"

Henry and Peter *glared* at each other.

"Okay," said **Horrid Henry**. "I won't invade your room if you won't invade mine."

"Okay," said Perfect Peter. He'd agree to anything to get Henry to leave his sheep alone.

Horrid Henry smirked.
He couldn't wait until tomorrow when Peter tried to play his cello . . . tee hee. Wouldn't he get a shock!

MOODY
MARGARET'S
SLEEPOVER

"What are you doing here?" said Moody Margaret, glaring.

"I'm here for the sleepover," said Sour Susan, glaring back.

"You were uninvited, remember?" said Margaret.

"And then you invited me again, remember?" snapped Susan.

"**Did not**."

"Did too. You told me last week I could come."

"Didn't."

"Did. You're such a MEANIE, Margaret," scowled Susan.

AAAARRGGGHH. Why was she

friends with such a **MOODY OLD GROUCH?**

MOODY MARGARET heaved a heavy sigh.
Why was she friends with such a
sour old *slop bucket*?

"Well, since you're here, I guess
you'd better come in," said Margaret.
"But don't expect any dessert 'cause
there won't be enough for you and my
real guests."

Sour Susan *stomped* inside
Margaret's house. Grrrr. She wouldn't
be inviting Margaret to her next
sleepover party, that's for sure.

Horrid Henry couldn't sleep. He was hot. He was hungry.

"Biscuits!" moaned his tummy. "Give me biscuits!"

Because Mum and Dad were the MEANEST, most HORRIBLE parents in the world, they'd forgotten to buy more biscuits and there wasn't a SINGLE SOLITARY CRUMB in the house. Henry knew because he'd searched everywhere.

"GIVE ME BISCUITS!" growled his tummy. "What are you waiting for?"

I'm going to die of hunger up here, thought **Horrid Henry**. And it will be all Mum and Dad's fault. They'll come in tomorrow morning and find just a few WISPS of hair and some teeth. Then they'd be sorry. Then they'd wail and gnash. But it would be too late.

"How could we have forgotten to buy chocolate biscuits?" Dad would sob.

"We deserve to be locked up for ever!" Mum would shriek.

"And now there's nothing left of Henry but a tooth, and it's all our fault!" they'd howl.

Humph. Serve them right.

Wait. What an idiot he was. Why should he risk **DEATH** from starvation when he knew where there was a rich stash of all sorts of **YUMMY** biscuits waiting just for him?

MOODY MARGARET'S SECRET CLUB tent was sure to be full to bursting with goodies! **Horrid Henry** hadn't raided it in ages. And so long as he was quick, no one would ever know he'd left the house.

"Go on, Henry," urged his tummy. **FEED ME!**

Horrid Henry didn't need to be urged twice. Slowly, quietly, he SNEAKED out of bed, crept down the stairs, and tiptoed out of the back door. Then quick over the wall, and hey presto, he was in the Secret Club tent. There was MARGARET'S SECRET CLUB biscuit tin, in her pathetic hiding place under a blanket. HA!

Horrid Henry prised open the lid. Oh wow. It was filled to

the brim with **Chocolate Fudge Chewies!** And those scrumptious **TRIPLE CHOCOLATE CHIP MARSHMALLOW SQUIDGIES!** Henry scooped up a huge handful and stuffed them in his mouth.

CHOMP. CHOMP. CHOMP.

Oh wow. Oh wow. Was there anything more delicious in the whole wide world than a mouthful of nicked biscuits?

"**MORE! MORE! MORE!**" yelped his tummy.

Who was **Horrid Henry** to say no?

Henry reached in to snatch another mega handful . . .

BANG! SLAM! BANG! STOMP! STOMP! STOMP!

"That's too bad, Gurinder," snapped Margaret's voice. "It's my party so I decide. Hurry up, Susan."

"I am hurrying," said Susan's voice.

The footsteps were heading straight for the SECRET CLUB tent.

Yikes. What was Margaret doing
outside at this time of night? There
wasn't a moment to lose.

Horrid Henry looked around
wildly. Where could he hide? There
was a wicker chest at the back,
where Margaret kept her dressing-up
clothes. Horrid Henry *leapt* inside and
pulled the lid shut. Hopefully, the
girls wouldn't be long and he could
escape home before Mum and Dad
discovered he'd been out.

MOODY MARGARET bustled into the tent, followed by her mother, Gorgeous Gurinder, Kung-Fu Kate, Lazy Linda, Vain Violet, Singing Soraya and Sour Susan.

"Now, girls, it's late, I want you to go straight to bed, lights out, no talking," said Margaret's mother. "My little Maggie Moo Moo needs her beauty sleep."

HA, thought Horrid Henry. Margaret could sleep for a thousand

years and she'd still look like a **frog**.

"Yes, Mum," said Margaret.

"Good night, girls," trilled
Margaret's mum. "See you in the
morning."

Phew, thought Horrid Henry, lying
as still as he could. He'd be back
home in no time, mission safely
accomplished.

"We're sleeping out here?" said

Singing Soraya. "In a tent?"

"I said it was a SECRET CLUB sleepover," said Margaret.

Horrid Henry's heart sank. Huh? They were planning to sleep here? RATS RATS RATS DOUBLE RATS. He was going to have to hide inside this hot dusty chest until they were asleep.

Maybe they'll all fall asleep soon, thought Horrid Henry hopefully.

Because he had to get home before Mum and Dad discovered he was missing. If they realised he'd SNEAKED outside, he'd be in so much trouble his life wouldn't be worth living and he might as well abandon all hope of ever watching 𝕋𝕍 or eating another biscuit until he was an **old, shrivelled bag of bones** struggling to chew with his one tooth and watch telly with his magnifying glass and hearing aid. Yikes!

Horrid Henry looked grimly at the

biscuits clutched in his fist. Thank goodness he'd brought provisions. He might be trapped here for a very long time.

"Where's your sleeping bag, Violet?" said Margaret.

"I didn't bring one," said Vain Violet. "I don't like sleeping on the floor."

"**Tough**," said Margaret, "that's where we're sleeping."

"But I need to sleep in a bed," whined Vain Violet. "I don't want to sleep out here."

"Well, we do," said Margaret.

"Yeah," said Susan.

"I can sleep anywhere," said Lazy Linda, yawning.

"I'm calling my mum," said Violet. **"I want to go home**."

"Go ahead," said Margaret. "We don't need you, do we?"

Silence.

"Oh go on, Violet, stay," said Gurinder.

"Yeah, stay," said Kung-Fu Kate.

"No!" said Violet, *flouncing* out of the tent.

"Hummph," said Moody Margaret. "She's no fun anyway. Now, everyone put your sleeping bags down where I say. I need to sleep by the entrance, because I need *fresh air*."

"I want to sleep by the entrance," said Soraya.

"No," said Margaret, "it's my party so I decide. Susan, you go at the back because you snore."

"Do not," said Susan.

"Do too," said Margaret.

"Liar."

"Liar."

SLAP!

SLAP!

"That's it!" wailed Susan. "I'm calling my mum."

"Go ahead," said Margaret, "see if I care, snore-box. That'll be loads more **Chocolate Fudge Chewies** for the rest of us."

Sour Susan stood still. She'd been looking forward to Margaret's sleepover for ages. And she still hadn't had any of the **MIDNIGHT FEAST** Margaret had promised.

"All right, I'll stay," said Susan sourly, putting her sleeping bag down at the back of the tent by the dressing-up chest.

"I want to be next to Gurinder," said Lazy Linda, scratching her head.

"Do you have **NITS?**" said Gurinder.

"No!" said Linda.

"You do too," said Gurinder.

"Do not," said Linda.

"Do too," said Gurinder. "I'm not sleeping next to someone who has nits."

"Me neither," said Kate.

"Me neither," said Soraya.

"Don't look at me," said Margaret. "I'm not sleeping next to you."

"I don't have nits!" wailed Linda.

"Go next to Susan," said Margaret.

"But she snores," protested Linda.

"But she has nits," protested Susan.

"Do not."

"Do not."

Snory!"

"**NiTTy!**"

Suddenly something scuttled across the floor.

"EEEEK!" squealed Soraya. "It's a mouse!" She scrambled on to the dressing-up chest. The lid sagged.

"It won't hurt you," said Margaret.

"Yeah," said Susan.

"EEEEK!" squealed Linda, shrinking back.

The lid sagged even more.

CREE—EAAAK went the chest.

Aaarrrrgggghhh, thought **Horrid Henry**, trying to squash himself down before he was squished.

"Eeeek!" squealed Gurinder, scrambling on to the chest.

CREE—EAAAAAK! went the chest.

Errrrgh, thought **Horrid Henry**,

pushing up against the sagging lid as hard as he could.

"I can't sleep if there's a . . . mouse," said Gurinder. She looked around nervously. "What if it runs on top of my sleeping bag?"

Margaret sighed. "It's only a mouse," she said.

"I'm scared of mice," whimpered Gurinder. "I'm leaving!" And she ran out of the tent, wailing.

"More food for the rest of us," said Margaret, shrugging. "I say we feast now."

"About time," said Soraya.

"Let's start with the **Chocolate Fudge Chewies**," said Margaret, opening the SECRET CLUB biscuit tin. "Everyone can have two, except for me, I get four 'cause it's my . . ."

Margaret peered into the tin. There were only a few crumbs inside.

"Who stole the biscuits?" said Margaret.

"Wasn't me," said Susan.

"Wasn't me," said Soraya.

"Wasn't me," said Kate.

"Wasn't me," said Linda.

TEE HEE, thought **Horrid Henry**.

"One of you did, so no one is getting anything to eat until you admit it," snapped Margaret.

"**MEANIE**," muttered Susan sourly.

"What did you say?" said Moody Margaret.

"Nothing," said Susan.

"Then we'll just have to wait for the culprit to come forward," said Margaret, scowling. "Meanwhile, get into your sleeping bags. We're going

to tell *scary* stories in the dark. Who
knows a good one?"

"I do," said Susan.

"Not the story about the ghost
kitty-cat which
drank up all
the milk in
your kitchen,
is it?" said
Margaret.

Susan
scowled.

"Well, it's a true *scary*
story," said Susan.

"I know a real scary story," said Kung-Fu Kate. "It's about this **MONSTER**—"

"Mine's better," said Margaret. "It's about a **flesh-eating zombie** which creeps around at night and rips off—"

"**NOoOo**," wailed Linda. "I hate being scared. I'm calling my mum to come and get me."

"No scaredy-cats allowed in the Secret Club," said Margaret.

"I don't care," said Linda, *flouncing* out.

"It's not a sleepover unless we tell **GHOST** stories," said Moody Margaret. "Turn off your torches. It won't be scary unless we're all sitting in the dark."

SNIFFLE. SNIFFLE. SNIFFLE.

"I want to go home," snivelled Soraya. "I've never slept away from home before ... I want my mummy."

"What a baby," said Moody Margaret.

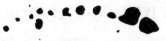

Horrid Henry was cramped and hot

and uncomfortable. Pins and needles were shooting up his arm. He shifted his shoulder, brushing against the lid.

There was a muffled **creak**.

Henry froze. Whoops. Henry prayed they hadn't heard anything.

". . . and the **zombie** crept inside the tent gnashing its bloody teeth and sniffing the air for human flesh, hungry for more—"

Ow. His poor aching arm. Henry shifted position again.

Creak . . .

"What was that?" whispered Susan.

"What was what?" said Margaret.

"There was a . . . a . . . creak . . ."
said Susan.

"The wind," said Margaret.
"Anyway, the **zombie** sneaked into
the tent and—"

"You don't think . . ." hissed Kate.

"Think what?" said Margaret.

"That the zombie . . . the zombie . . ."

I'm starving, thought Horrid Henry.
I'll just eat a few biscuits really,
really, really quietly—

CRUNCH. CRUNCH.

"What was that?" whispered Susan.

"What was what?" said Margaret.
"You're ruining the story."

"That . . . crunching sound," hissed
Susan.

Horrid Henry gasped. What an
idiot he was! Why hadn't he thought
of this before?

CRUNCH. CRUNCH. CRUNCH.

"Like someone . . . someone . . . crunching on . . . bones," whispered Kung-Fu Kate.

"Someone . . . here . . ." whispered Susan.

TAP. **Horrid Henry** rapped on the underside of the lid.

TAP! TAP! TAP!

"I didn't hear anything," said Margaret loudly.

"It's the **zombie!**" screamed Susan.

"He's in here!" screamed Kate. **"AAAAARRRRRRRGHHHHHHH!"**

"I'm going home!" screamed Susan and Kate. "MUMMMMMMMMMYYYY!" they wailed, running off.

Ha ha, thought **Horrid Henry**. His *brilliant* plan had worked!!! **TEE HEE**. He'd hop out, steal the rest of the feast and scoot home. Hopefully Mum and Dad—

YANK!

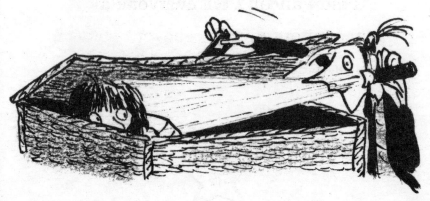

Suddenly the chest lid was flung open and a torch shone in his eyes. MOODY MARGARET's hideous face *glared* down at him.

"Gotcha!" said Moody Margaret. "Oh boy, are you in trouble. Just wait till I tell on you. HA HA, Henry, you're dead."

Horrid Henry climbed out of the chest and brushed a few crumbs on to the carpet.

"Just wait till I tell everyone at school about your sleepover," said Horrid Henry. "How you were so

MEAN and **BOSSY** everyone ran away."

"Your parents will punish you for ever," said Moody Margaret.

"Your name will be mud for ever," said Horrid Henry. "Everyone will laugh at you and it serves you right, Maggie Moo Moo."

"Don't call me that," said Margaret, glaring.

"Call you what, Moo Moo?"

"All right," said Margaret slowly. "I won't tell on you if you give me **TWO** packs of **Chocolate Fudge Chewies**."

"No way," said Henry. "I won't tell on you if you give me **three** packs of **Chocolate Fudge Chewies**."

"Fine," said Margaret. "Your parents are still up. I'll tell them where you are right now. I wouldn't want them to worry."

"Go ahead," said Henry. "I can't wait until school tomorrow."

Margaret scowled.

"Just this once," said Horrid Henry. "I won't tell on you if you won't tell on me."

"Just this once," said Moody

Margaret. "But never again."

They *glared* at each other.

When he was king, thought Horrid Henry, anyone named Margaret would be catapulted over the walls into an oozy swamp. Meanwhile . . . on guard, Margaret. On guard. I will be avenged!

HORRID HENRY'S
AUTOBIOGRAPHY

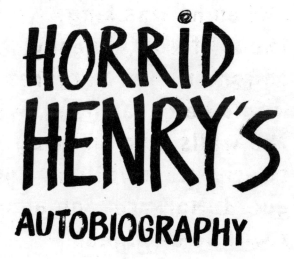

BANG! CRASH! Kaboom!

Rude Ralph bounced on a chair and did his Tarzan impression.

Moody Margaret yanked Lazy Linda's hair. Linda screamed.

Stone-Age Steven stomped round the room grunting "Ugg."

"Rat about town

don't need a gown.

Where I'm goin'

Only fangs'll be showin',"

shrieked Horrid Henry.

"**Quiet!**" barked **MISS BATTLE-AXE**. "Settle down immediately."

Ralph bounced.

Steven **stomped**.

Linda screamed.

Henry **SHRIEKED**. He was the
Killer Boy Rats' new lead singer,
blasting his music into the roaring
crowd, hurling—

"HENRY, BE QUIET!"
bellowed Miss Battle-Axe. "Or
playtime is cancelled. For everyone."

Horrid Henry scowled. Why oh
why did he have to come to school?
Why didn't the **Killer Boy Rats** start
a school, where you'd do nothing but

SCREAM and **stomp**
all day? Now that's
the sort of school
everyone would
want to go to. But
no. He had to come
here. When he was king, all schools
would just teach jousting and spying
and **Terminator Gladiator** would
be Head.

Henry looked at the clock. How
could it be only 9.42? It felt like he'd
been sitting here for ages. What he'd
give to be lounging right now on the

comfy **BLACK** chair, eating crisps and watching **Hog House** . . .

"Today we have a very exciting project," said **MISS BATTLE-AXE**.

Henry groaned. Miss Battle-Axe's idea of an **EXCITING** project and his were never the same. An exciting project would be building a time machine, or a let's see who can give Henry the most **CHOCOLATE** competition, or counting how many times he could hit Miss Battle-Axe with a **water balloon**.

"We'll be writing autobiographies,"

said Miss Battle-Axe.

Ha. He knew it would be something
boring. **Horrid Henry** hated writing.
All that *pushing* a pen across a piece
of paper. Writing always made his
hand ache. Writing was hard, heavy
work. Why did **MISS BATTLE-AXE** try to
TORTURE him every day? Didn't she
have anything better to do? Henry
groaned again.

"An *autobiography* means the story of your life," continued Miss Battle-Axe, *glaring* at him with her evil red eyes. "Everyone will write a page about themselves and all the interesting things they've done."

Yawn. Could his life get any WORSE?

Write a page? A whole entire page? What could be more BORING than writing on and on about HIMSELF—

Wait a minute.

He got to write . . . about HIMSELF? The world's most FASCINATING boy? He could write for hours about

himself! Days. Weeks. Years. Hold on
. . . what was batty old **MISS BATTLE-AXE**
saying now?

". . . the really exciting part is that
our autobiographies will be published
in the local newspaper next week."

**oh wow! oh wow! oh
wow!** His *autobiography* would be
published!

This was his chance to tell the
world all about being *Lord High
Excellent Majesty of the Purple
Hand Gang*. How he'd vanquished
so many evil enemies. All the *brilliant*

tricks he'd played on Peter. He'd write about the Mega-Mean Time Machine. And the Fangmangler. And the millions of times he'd defeated the SECRET CLUB and squished MOODY MARGARET to a pulp! And oh yes, he'd be sure to include the time he'd turned his one line in the school play into a starring part and scored the winning goal in the class football match. But one page would barely cover one day in his life. He needed HUNDREDS of pages . . . no, THOUSANDS of pages to write about just some of his **TOP TRIUMPHS**.

Where to begin?

"Let's start with you, Clare," burbled
Miss Battle-Axe. "What would you
put in your *autobiography*?"

Clare beamed. "I walked when I
was four months old, learned to read
when I was two, did long division
when I was three, built my first
telescope when I was four, composed
a *symphony*—"

"Thank you, Clare, I'm sure everyone will look forward to learning more about you," said **MISS BATTLE-AXE**. "Steven. What will—"

"Can't we just get started?" shouted Henry. "I've got **MASSES** to write."

"As I was saying, before I was so **RUDELY** interrupted," said Miss Battle-Axe, *glaring*, "Steven, what will you be writing about in your *autobiography*?"

"Being a caveman," grunted Stone-Age Steven. "**Uggg**."

"Fascinating," said **MISS BATTLE-AXE**. "Bert! What's interesting about your life?"

"I dunno," said Beefy Bert.

"Right, then, everyone get to work," said Miss Battle-Axe, fixing Horrid Henry with her basilisk stare.

Horrid Henry wrote until his hand ached. But he'd barely got to the time he tricked Margaret into eating **GLOP** before **MISS BATTLE-AXE** ordered everyone to stop.

"But I haven't finished!" shouted Horrid Henry.

"**TOUGH**," said Miss Battle-Axe. "Now, before we send these autobiographies to the newspaper, I'd like a few of you to read yours aloud to the class. William, let's start with you."

Weepy William burst into tears. "I don't want to go first," he wailed, dabbing his eyes with some loo paper.

"Read," said Miss Battle-Axe.

WILLIAM'S AUTOBIOGRAPHY

I was born. I cried. A few years later my brother Neil was born. I cried.

In school Toby broke my

pencil. Margaret picked me last. When we had to build the Parthenon Henry took all my paper and then when I got some more it was dirty. I had to play a blade of grass in the Nativity play. I cried.

I lost every race on Sports Day.

I cried. Then I got nits. On the school trip to the Ice Cream Factory I did a wee in my pants. I cried. Nothing else has ever happened to me.

"Who's next?" asked Miss Battle-Axe.

Horrid Henry's hand shot up.

MISS BATTLE-AXE looked as if a zombie had just walked across

her grave. **Horrid Henry** never put
his hand up.

"Linda," said Miss Battle-Axe.

Lazy Linda woke up and yawned.

LINDA'S AUTOBIOGRAPHY

I've had many nice beds in my life.
First was my Moses basket. Then my cot.
Then my little bed. Then my great big
sleigh bed. Then my princess bed with the
curtains and the yellow headboard. I've

also had a lot of duvets. First my duvet had ducks on it. Then I got a new soft one with big fluffy clouds. Oooh, I am sleepy just thinking about it ...

"We have time to hear one more," said **MISS BATTLE-AXE**, scanning the class. **Horrid Henry** thought his arm would detach itself from his shoulder if he shoved it any higher. "Margaret," said Miss Battle-Axe.

Henry scowled. It was so unfair. No one wanted to know about that moody old grouch.

MOODY MARGARET swaggered
to the front and noisily
cleared her throat.

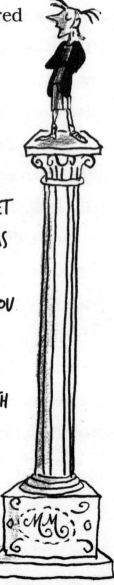

<u>MARGARET'S AUTOBIOGRAPHY</u>

GREETINGS, WORLD. I'M VERY SAD
WHEN I THINK THAT MANY OF
YOU READING THIS WILL NEVER GET
TO MEET SOMEONE AS AMAZING AS
ME. BUT AT LEAST YOU CAN READ
SOMETHING I'VE WRITTEN, AND YOU
NEWSPAPER PEOPLE SHOULD SAVE
THIS PIECE OF PAPER, BECAUSE I,
MARGARET, HAVE TOUCHED IT WITH
MY VERY OWN HANDS, AND IT'S

SURE TO BE VALUABLE IN THE FUTURE WHEN I'M FAMOUS.

LET ME TELL YOU A FEW THINGS ABOUT MARVELLOUS ME. FIRST, I AM THE LEADER OF THE SECRET CLUB, WHICH IS ALWAYS VICTORIOUS AGAINST THE PATHETIC AND PUNY PURPLE HAND GANG NEXT DOOR. ONE REASON WE ALWAYS DESTROY THEM, APART FROM MY BRILLIANT PLOTTING, IS BECAUSE THE PURPLE HAND'S SO-CALLED LEADER, HENRY, IS REALLY STUPID AND USELESS AND PATHETIC.

Horrid Henry could not believe his ears.

97

"**LIAR!**" shouted Henry. "I always win!"

"Shh!" said **MISS BATTLE-AXE**.

NATURALLY, I AM THE BEST FOOTBALLER THE SCHOOL HAS EVER HAD OR WILL EVER HAVE, AND NATURALLY I'M CAPTAIN OF THE FOOTBALL TEAM. EVERYONE ALWAYS WANTS TO PLAY ON MY TEAM, BUT OF COURSE I DON'T LET NO-HOPERS LIKE HENRY ON IT. I'M ALSO A FANTASTIC TRUMPET PLAYER, AND A TOP SPY. MY BEST TOY IS MY DUNGEON DRINK KIT, WHICH I'VE USED MANY TIMES TO PLAY GREAT TRICKS ON THE PURPLE HAND GANG, WHICH THEY ALWAYS FALL FOR.

BUT I KNOW I'LL BE VERY FAMOUS SO I'M SAVING MY BEST STORIES FOR MY FUTURE BEST-SELLING AUTOBIOGRAPHY. I EXPECT THERE WILL BE MANY STATUES OF ME BUILT ALL OVER TOWN, AND THAT THIS SCHOOL WILL BE RENAMED THE MARGARET SCHOOL.

I KNOW IT'S HARD REALISING THAT YOU CAN NEVER BE AS GREAT AS ME, BUT GET USED TO IT!!!

MOODY MARGARET stopped reading and swaggered to her seat.

"Yay!" yelled Sour Susan.

"**Boo!**" yelled Horrid Henry.

"Boo!" yelled Rude Ralph.

"There's no booing in this class," said Miss Battle-Axe.

Horrid Henry was outraged. Margaret's lies about him . . . published? The Purple Hand Gang always won. But the whole world would believe her lies once they read them in a newspaper. He had to stop that foul fiend. He had to show everyone what a *pants-face liar* Margaret really was.

But how? How? He could just try to

steal her *autobiography*. But someone
might notice it had gone missing. Or
he could . . . he could . . .

The playtime bell rang. **MISS BATTLE-
AXE** started collecting up all the
autobiographies. Henry watched

helplessly as Margaret's pack of boasting lies went into the folder.

And then **Horrid Henry** knew what he had to do. It was **DANGEROUS**. It was risky. But a **PIRATE GANG LEADER** had to take his chances, come what may.

Horrid Henry put up his hand. "Please, miss, I haven't finished my *autobiography* yet. Could I stay in at playtime to finish?"

MISS BATTLE-AXE looked at Henry as if he had just grown an extra head. Henry . . . asking to spend more time on work? **Horrid Henry**

asking to skip playtime?

"You can have five more minutes," said Miss Battle-Axe, mopping her brow.

Horrid Henry wrote and wrote and wrote. When would **MISS BATTLE-AXE** leave him alone for a moment? But there she was, stapling up drawings of light bulbs.

"Put it in the folder with the others," said Miss Battle-Axe, facing the wall. **Horrid Henry** didn't wait to be asked twice and grabbed the folder. There wasn't a moment to lose. Henry rifled through the autobiographies, removed

Margaret's, and substituted his new, improved version.

MOODY MARGARET peered round the door. TEE HEE, thought **Horrid Henry**, pushing past her. Wouldn't she get a shock when she got her newspaper! What he'd give to see her face.

THWACK!

The local paper **dropped** through

the door. Henry snatched it. There was the headline:

LOCAL CHILDREN SHINE IN FASCINATING TALES OF THEIR LIVES

Feverishly, he turned to read the class autobiographies.

MARGARET'S AUTOBIOGRAPHY

Oh woe is me, to be such a silly moody grouchy grump. I've always looked like a frog, in fact my mum took one look at me when I was born, threw me in the bin and ran screaming from the room. I don't blame her; I scream too whenever I see my ugly warty face in the mirror. Everyone calls me Maggie Moo

Moo, or Maggie Poo Poo, because I still wear
nappies. I started a Secret Club, which no one
wants to join, because I am so mean and bossy.
I can't even have a sleepover without everyone
running away. I keep trying to beat Henry's
Purple Hand Gang, but he's much too clever for
me and always foils my evil plans. I live next
door to Henry, but of course I don't deserve such
a great honour. I really should just live in a
smelly hole somewhere with all the other frogs.
So, just remember, everyone, beware of being a
moody, grouchy grump, or you might end up as
horrible as me.

Yes! What a triumph!
He was brilliant. He
was a genius. What
an amazing trick

to write the truth about Margaret
and swap it for her pack of lies.

Horrid Henry beamed. Now to
enjoy his own *autobiography*. It was
far too short, but there was always
next time.

Henry's AUTOBIOGRAPHY

I'm a total copycat. Luckily, I live next door
to the amazing Margaret, who I look up to and
admire and worship more than anyone in the
world. Margaret is my heroine, but I will never
be as clever or as brilliant as she is, because I'm
a pathetic, useless toad. I copied her amazing

Secret Club, but the Purple Hand always loses. I tried to do makeovers, but of course I couldn't. Even my own brother wants to work for her as a spy. But then, she is an empress and I'm a worm.

The most exciting thing that ever happened to me was when Margaret moved in next door. I hope that one day she will let me be the guard of the Secret Club, but I will have to work very hard to deserve it. That would be the best thing that has ever happened in my boring life.

Huh? What? That fiend!
That foul fiend!

The doorbell rang.

There was Margaret, waving the newspaper. Her face was purple.

"How dare you!" she shrieked.

"How dare you!" Henry shrieked.

"I'll get you for this, Henry," hissed Margaret.

"Just you wait, Margaret," hissed Henry.

HORRID HENRY

ROCK STAR

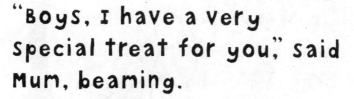

"Boys, I have a very special treat for you," said Mum, beaming.

Horrid Henry looked up from his Mutant Max comic.

Perfect Peter looked up from his spelling homework.

A treat? A **special** treat? A VERY SPECIAL treat? Maybe Mum and Dad were finally appreciating him. Maybe they'd got tickets . . . maybe they'd actually got tickets . . . Horrid Henry's heart leapt. Could it be possible that at last, at long last, he'd get to go to a **Killer Boy Rats** concert?

"We're going to the **Daffy and her Dancing Daisies** show!" said Mum. "I got the last four tickets."

"OOOOOOHHHH," said Peter, clapping his hands. "**YIPPEE!** I love Daffy."

what?? NOOOOOOOOOOO! That wasn't a treat. That was **TORTURE**. A treat would be a day at the **FROSTY FREEZE ICE CREAM FACTORY**. A treat would be no school. A treat would be all he could eat at **Gobble and Go**.

"I don't want to see that stupid Daffy," said Horrid Henry. "I want to see the **Killer Boy Rats**."

"No way," said Mum.

"I don't like the **Killer Boy Rats**," shuddered Peter. "Too scary."

"Me neither," shuddered Mum. "Too loud."

"Me neither," shuddered Dad. "Too **SHOUTY**."

"**NOOOOOOOO!**" screamed Henry.

"But Henry," said Peter, "everyone loves Daffy."

"Not me," snarled Henry.

Daffy sings and dances her way across the stage and into your heart. Your chance to sing along to all your favourite daisy songs! I'm a Lazy Daisy. Whoops-a-Daisy. And of course, Upsy-Daisy, Crazy Daisy, Prance and Dance-a-Daisy.

With special guest star Busy Lizzie!!!

Perfect Peter waved a leaflet. "Daffy's going to be the **GREATEST SHOW EVER**. Read this."

AAAAARRRRRGGGGGHHHHHH.

Moody Margaret's parents were taking her to the **Killer Boy Rats** concert. Rude Ralph was going to

the **Killer Boy Rats**
concert. Even Anxious
Andrew was going,
and he didn't even like
them. **STUCK-UP STEVE** had

been bragging for months that he
was going and would be sitting in a
special box. It was so unfair.

No one was a bigger **Rats** fan than
Horrid Henry. Henry had all their
albums: *Killer Boy Rats Attack-Tack-Tack*, *Killer Boy Rats Splat!* and
Killer Boy Rats Manic Panic.

"**IT'S NOT FAIR!**" screamed Horrid Henry. "I want to see the Killers!!!!"

"We have to see something that everyone in the family will like," said Mum. "Peter's too young for the **Killer Boy Rats** but we can all enjoy Daffy."

"Not me!" screamed Henry.

Oh, why did he have such a stupid nappy baby for a brother? Younger brothers should be banned. They just wrecked everything. When he was **KING HENRY THE HORRIBLE**, all younger brothers would be

arrested and dumped in a volcano.

In fact, why wait?

Horrid Henry pounced. He was a fiery god scooping up a human sacrifice and hurling him into the volcano's molten depths.

"AAAIIIIIEEEEEEE!" screamed Perfect Peter. "Henry attacked me."

"Stop being **HORRID**, Henry!" shouted Mum. "Leave your brother alone."

"I won't go to Daffy," yelled Henry.
"And you can't make me."

"Go to your room," said Dad.

Horrid Henry paced up and down his bedroom, singing his favourite Rats song at the top of his lungs:
"I'M DEAD, YOU'RE DEAD, WE'RE DEAD. GET OVER IT.
DEAD IS GREAT, DEAD'S WHERE IT'S AT 'CAUSE . . ."

"Henry! Be quiet!" screamed Dad.

"I am being quiet!" bellowed Henry.

Honestly. Now, how could he get out of going to that terrible Daffy concert? He'd easily be the oldest one there. Only **STUPID** babies liked Daffy. If the **horrible** songs didn't kill him then he was sure to die of embarrassment. Then they'd be sorry they'd made him go. But it would be too late. Mum and Dad and Peter could sob and **boo hoo** all they liked but he'd still be dead. And serve them right for being so mean to him.

Dad said if he was good he could see the **Killer Boys** next time they

were in town. Ha. The **Killer Boy Rats**
NEVER gave concerts. Next time they
did he'd be old and hobbling and
whacking Peter with his cane.

He had to get a **Killer Boys** ticket
now. He just had to. But how? They'd
been sold out for weeks.

Maybe he could place an ad:

CAN YOU HELP?
DESERVING BOY SUFFERING FROM RARE AND TERRIBLE
ILLNESS. HIS EARS ARE FALLING OFF. DOCTOR HAS PRESCRIBED
THE KILLER BOY RATS CURE. ONLY BY HEARING THE RATS
LIVE IS THERE ANY HOPE. IF YOU'VE GOT A TICKET TO THE
CONCERT ON SATURDAY PLEASE SEND IT TO HENRY NOW.
(IF YOU DON'T YOU KNOW YOU'LL BE SORRY.)

That might work. Or he could tell people that the concert was CURSED and anyone who went would turn into a rat. Hmmm. Somehow Henry didn't see Margaret falling for that. Too bad Peter didn't have a ticket, thought Henry sadly, he could tell him he'd turn into a killer and Peter would hand over the ticket instantly.

And then suddenly **Horrid Henry** had a *brilliant*, **SPECTACULAR** idea. There must be someone out there who was desperate for a Daffy ticket. In fact there must be someone out there who would swap a Killers ticket for a Daffy one. It was certainly worth a try.

"Hey, Brian, I hear you've got a **Killer Boy Rats** ticket," said Horrid Henry at school the next day.

"So?" said Brainy Brian.

"I've got a ticket to something much better," said Henry.

"What?" said Brian. "The Killers are the best."

Horrid Henry could barely force the grisly words out of his mouth. He twisted his lips into a smile.

"Daffy and her Dancing Daisies," said Horrid Henry.

Brainy Brian stared at him.

"Daffy and her Dancing Daisies?" he spluttered.

"Yes," said Horrid Henry brightly. "I've heard it's their BEST SHOW

EVER. Great new songs. You'd love it. Wanna swap?"

Brainy Brian stared at him as if he had a **TURNIP** instead of a head.

"You're trying to swap Daffy and her Dancing Daisies tickets for the Killer Boy Rats?" said Brian slowly.

"I'm doing you a favour, no one likes the Killer Boy Rats any more," said Henry.

"I do," said Brian.

RATS.

"How come you have a ticket for Daffy?" said Brian. "Isn't that a baby show?"

"It's not mine, I found it," said Horrid Henry quickly. **OOPS**.

"Ha ha, Henry, I'm seeing the Killers, and you're not," Margaret taunted.

"Yeah, Henry," said Sour Susan.

"I heard . . ." Margaret doubled over laughing, "I heard you were going to the Daffy show!"

"That's a **big fat lie**," said Henry

hotly. "I wouldn't be seen **DEAD**
there."

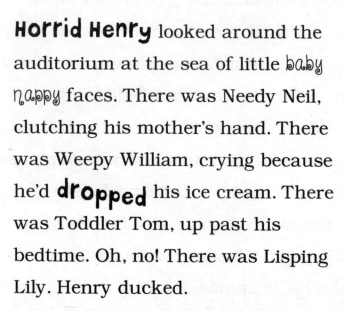

Horrid Henry looked around the
auditorium at the sea of little baby
nappy faces. There was Needy Neil,
clutching his mother's hand. There
was Weepy William, crying because
he'd **dropped** his ice cream. There
was Toddler Tom, up past his
bedtime. Oh, no! There was Lisping
Lily. Henry ducked.

Phew. She hadn't seen him.

Margaret would never stop teasing him if she ever found out. When he was *king*, Daffy and her Dancing Daisies would live in a **dungeon** with only **RATS** for company. Anyone who so much as mentioned the name Daffy, or even grew a daisy, would be flushed down the toilet.

There was a round of polite applause as Daffy and her Dancing Daisies pirouetted on stage. **Horrid Henry** slumped in his seat as far as he could slump and pulled his cap over his face. Thank goodness he'd come disguised and brought some earplugs. No one would ever know he'd been.

"TRA LA LA LA LA LA LA!" trilled the Daisies.

"TRA LA LA LA LA LA LA!" trilled the audience.

Oh, the torture, groaned **Horrid Henry** as **HORRIBLE** song followed horrible song. Perfect Peter sang along. So did Mum and Dad.

AAARRRRRGGGHHHHH.
And to think that tomorrow
night the Killer Boy Rats would be
performing . . . and he wouldn't be
there! It was so unfair.

Then Daffy cartwheeled to the
front of the stage. One of the daisies
stood beside her holding a giant hat.

"And now the moment all you
Daffy Daisy fans have been waiting
for," squealed Daffy. "It's the Lucky
Ducky Daisy Draw, when we call up
on stage an oh-so-lucky audience
member to lead us in the **Whoops-a-**

Daisy sing-along song! Who's it going to be?"

"Me!" squealed Peter. Mum squeezed his arm.

Daffy fumbled in the hat and pulled out a ticket.

"And the lucky winner of our ticket raffle is . . . **HENRY!** Ticket 597!

Ticket 597, yes Henry, you in row P, seat 10, come on up! Daffy needs you on stage!"

Horrid Henry was stuck to his seat in horror. It must be some other Henry. Never in his **WORST NIGHTMARES** had he ever imagined—

"Henry, that's you," said Perfect Peter. "You're so lucky."

"HENRY! COME ON UP, HENRY!" shrieked Daffy. "Don't be shy!"

On stage at the Daffy show? No! No! Wait till **MOODY MARGARET** found out. Wait till anyone found out. Henry would never hear the end of it. He wasn't moving. Pigs would fly before he budged.

"Henwy!" squealed Lisping Lily behind him. "Henwy! I want to give you a big kiss, Henwy . . ."

Horrid Henry leapt out of his seat. Lily! Lisping Lily! That fiend in toddler's clothing would stop at nothing to get hold of him. Before

Henry knew what had happened, ushers dressed as daisies had nabbed him and pushed him on stage.

Horrid Henry blinked in the lights. Was anyone in the world as unlucky as he?

"All together now, everyone get ready to ruffle their petals. Let's sing *Tippy-toe daisy do / Let us sing a song for you!*" beamed Daffy. "Henry, you start us off."

Horrid Henry stared at the vast audience. Everyone was looking at him. Of course he didn't know any

STUPID Daisy songs. He always blocked his ears or ran from the room whenever Peter sang them. Whatever could the words be . . .

> "Watch out, whoop-di-do
> Daisy's doing a big poo?"

These poor stupid kids. If only they could hear some decent songs, like . . . like . . .

> "GRANNY ON HER CRUTCHES
> PUSH HER OFF HER CHAIR
> SHOVE SHOVE SHOVE SHOVE
> SHOVE HER DOWN THE STAIRS!"

shrieked Horrid Henry.

The audience was silent. Daffy
looked stunned.

"Uh, Henry . . . that's not 𝒯𝒾𝓅𝓅𝓎-𝓉𝓸𝑒
𝒹𝒶𝒾𝓈𝓎 𝒹𝓸," whispered Daffy.

"C'mon everyone, join in with me,"
shouted Horrid Henry, spinning
round and twirling in his best

Killer Boy Rats manner.

> "I'M IN MY COFFIN
> NO TIME FOR COUGHIN'
> WHEN YOU'RE SQUISHED DOWN DEAD.
> DON'T CARE IF YOU'RE A BOFFIN
> DON'T CARE IF YOU'RE A LOONY,
> DON'T CARE IF YOU'RE CARTOONY
> I'LL SQUISH YOU!"

sang Horrid Henry as loud as he
could.

> "GONNA BE A ROCK STAR (AND YOU AIN'T)
> DON'T EVEN—"

Two security guards ran on stage
and grabbed **Horrid Henry**.

"Killer Boy Rats for ever!" shrieked Henry, as he was dragged off.

Horrid Henry *stared* at the special delivery letter covered in skulls and crossbones. His hand shook.

HEY HENRY,
WE SAW A VIDEO OF YOU SINGING OUR SONGS AND GETTING YANKED OFF STAGE – WAY TO GO, KILLER BOY! HERE'S A PAIR OF TICKETS FOR OUR CONCERT TONIGHT, AND A BACKSTAGE PASS – SEE YOU THERE.
            THE KILLER BOY RATS

Horrid Henry goggled at the tickets and the backstage pass. He couldn't move. He couldn't breathe. He was going to the **Killer Boy Rats** concert. He was actually going to the **Killer Boy Rats** concert.

Life, thought Horrid Henry, beaming, was sweet.

FOR MORE FIENDISH FUN READ

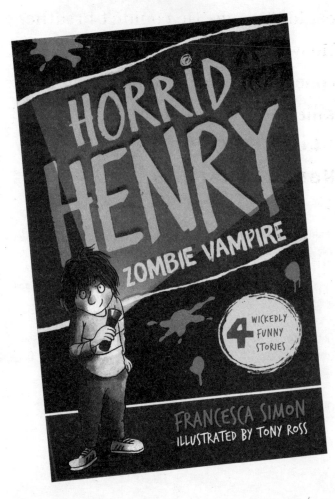

FRANCESCA SIMON

FRANCESCA SIMON SPENT HER CHILDHOOD ON THE BEACH IN CALIFORNIA AND STARTED WRITING STORIES AT THE AGE OF EIGHT. SHE WROTE HER FIRST HORRID HENRY BOOK IN 1994. HORRID HENRY HAS GONE ON TO CONQUER THE GLOBE; HIS ADVENTURES HAVE SOLD MILLIONS OF COPIES WORLDWIDE.

FRANCESCA HAS WON THE CHILDREN'S BOOK OF THE YEAR AWARD AND IN 2009 WAS AWARDED A GOLD BLUE PETER BADGE. SHE WAS ALSO A TRUSTEE OF THE WORLD BOOK DAY CHARITY FOR SIX YEARS.

FRANCESCA LIVES IN NORTH LONDON WITH HER FAMILY.

WWW.FRANCESCASIMON.COM
WWW.HORRIDHENRY.CO.UK
@SIMON_FRANCESCA

TONY ROSS

TONY ROSS WAS BORN IN LONDON AND STUDIED AT THE LIVERPOOL SCHOOL OF ART AND DESIGN. HE HAS WORKED AS A CARTOONIST, A GRAPHIC DESIGNER, AN ADVERTISING ART DIRECTOR AND A UNIVERSITY LECTURER.

TONY IS ONE OF THE MOST POPULAR AND SUCCESSFUL CHILDREN'S ILLUSTRATORS OF ALL TIME, BEST KNOWN FOR ILLUSTRATING HORRID HENRY AND THE WORKS OF DAVID WALLIAMS, AS WELL AS HIS OWN HUGELY POPULAR SERIES, THE LITTLE PRINCESS. HE LIVES IN MACCLESFIELD.

COLLECT ALL THE
HORRID HENRY STORYBOOKS!